KU-175-067

The Last Polar Bears

HARRY HORSE

PUFFIN BOOKS

RAIGMORE PRIMARY SCHOOL
INVERNESS

*Author's Apology:

My grandfather claims to have seen penguins on his journey
to the North Pole. He must have been mistaken, as it is
widely known that penguins are only to be found in
the South Pole.
For the purposes of this story, I have kept
the penguins in.
Roo says she wishes I had kept them out.

Harry Horse

For Mandy and Roo

PUFFIN BOOKS

Published by the Penguin Group
Penguin Books Ltd, 27 Wrights Lane, London W8 5TZ, England
Penguin Putnam Inc., 375 Hudson Street, New York, New York 10014, USA
Penguin Books Australia Ltd, Ringwood, Victoria, Australia
Penguin Books Canada Ltd, 10 Alcorn Avenue, Toronto, Ontario, Canada M4V 3B2
Penguin Books India (P) Ltd, 11 Community Centre, Panchsheel Park, New Delhi – 110 017, India
Penguin Books (NZ) Ltd, Cnr Rosedale and Airborne Roads, Albany, Auckland, New Zealand
Penguin Books (South Africa) (Pty) Ltd, 5 Watkins Street, Denver Ext 4, Johannesburg 2094, South Africa

Penguin Books Ltd, Registered Offices: Harmondsworth, Middlesex, England

On the World Wide Web at: www.penguin.com

This edition, based on *The Last Polar Bears* published by Viking 1993, published by Viking 2000
Published in Puffin Books 2001
1 3 5 7 9 10 8 6 4 2

Copyright © Harry Horse, 1993, 2000
All rights reserved

The moral right of the author/illustrator has been asserted

Filmset in Bembo 17/21pt

Printed in Dubai by Oriental Press

Except in the United States of America, this book is sold subject to the condition that it shall not,
by way of trade or otherwise, be lent, re-sold, hired out, or otherwise circulated without the publisher's
prior consent in any form of binding or cover other than that in which it is published and without
a similar condition including this condition being imposed on the subsequent purchaser

British Library Cataloguing in Publication Data
A CIP catalogue record for this book is available from the British Library

ISBN 0–140–56712–7

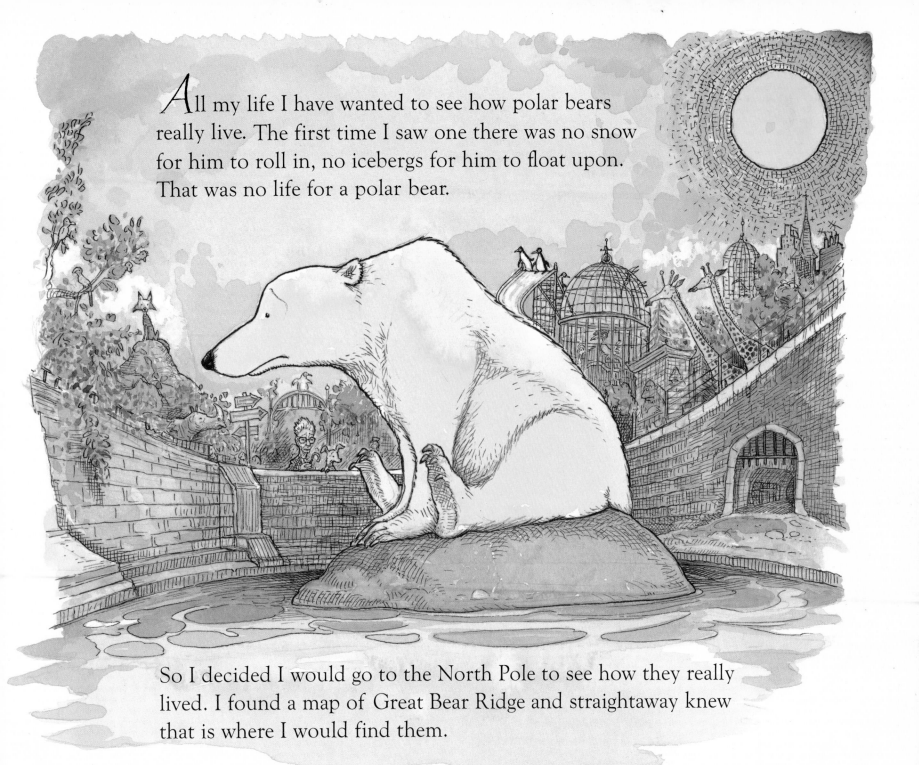

All my life I have wanted to see how polar bears really live. The first time I saw one there was no snow for him to roll in, no icebergs for him to float upon. That was no life for a polar bear.

So I decided I would go to the North Pole to see how they really lived. I found a map of Great Bear Ridge and straightaway knew that is where I would find them.

I wanted to buy a husky and a sledge to drag my equipment across the snow. But they cost too much money. In the end, I had to take Roo and a golf trolley. Roo said her breed were good on snow. Better than huskies probably.

I loaded the golf trolley with all the things we would need for our journey.

We crept out of the house and set sail for the North Pole on a ship called *The Unsinkable*.

Our cabin had two portholes, one for
Roo and one for me. I saw a whale.
Roo said she saw a sheep.

It took Roo a while to get used to being on a ship.
She lost her ball overboard and I had to tie her to
the mast to stop her jumping in after it.

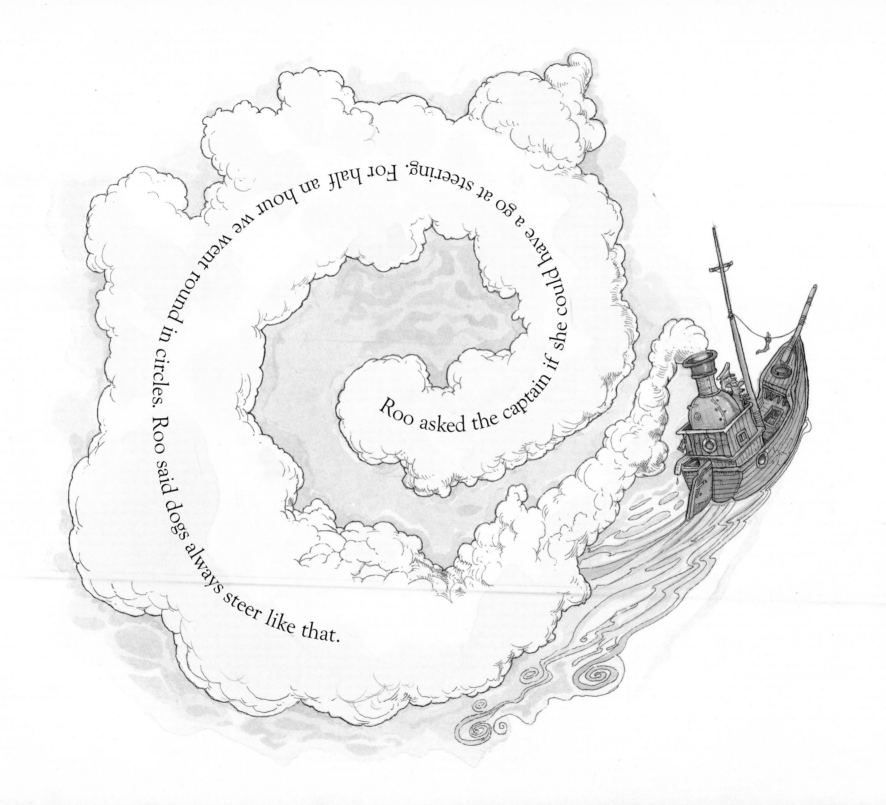

Roo asked the captain if she could have a go at steering. For half an hour we went round in circles. Roo said dogs always steer like that.

It was a long way to the North Pole. We sailed through storms and high seas and it grew colder and colder. Roo wore my socks to keep her paws warm.

Every day, Roo asked if we were there yet.
Every day, I had to tell her, not yet, but soon, very soon.

Then one night, the ship took a real pounding from a dreadful storm.

The engine stopped completely and when the captain tried to get it going again ...

nothing happened ...

until Roo helped.

Hurrah!!! At last we landed at a place called Walrus Bay. The captain wished me luck and gave Roo a tin of macaroni cheese. I think he really liked her. We were sad to see him go.

We were welcomed into Walrus by hundreds of penguins –
but no polar bears.

Our cabin stood on a hill just outside Walrus. It was very dirty inside and it seemed quite gloomy, but we soon cleaned it up.

It wasn't much, but it was home.

Our first night at the North Pole was very cold. Roo would not sleep in her basket and got into my bed. Her paws stuck into me and she fidgeted about so much I hardly slept a wink.

To make matters worse, a wolf sat on our roof and howled all night.

The next day, I wanted to begin our search for the
polar bears, but the snow kept on falling.

It snowed so much that it almost buried our cabin.

For three days we were cooped up and our fuel ran low.

I had to burn the chairs and Roo's basket to keep us warm.
Roo was very upset about her basket. She said that she wanted
to keep things in it. I said it was a pity she hadn't slept in it.
Sometimes I wish I had brought a husky.

I tried to sleep but was woken by more wolves running across the roof. Roo said that she was tired of looking for polar bears and wanted to go home. She said that it was sand her breed were good on. Not snow.

At last it stopped snowing and I took Roo out to a place called the Gentle Slopes. There she could practise pulling the golf trolley through the snow.

However, halfway up the slope, Roo decided she wanted to go down … and took off, dragging my golf trolley behind her. I was so angry with Roo that when we got home I didn't speak to her for ages.

In the end, she looked so sorry that I had to tell her the Great Bear Ridge ice cream story to cheer her up.

Once upon a time, I told her, the snow was so pure and clean that it tasted better than the finest ice cream. But as the air got dirtier from all the chemicals and fumes, the snow lost its taste. The last of the world's ice cream lies up on the Great Bear Ridge. And that is why we are going there. To get ice cream for Roo.

Roo loves this story. I have told it to her many times. I must admit I have added bits. The fabulous chocolate mint chip that grows in the shade or the delicious strawberry split found only at sunset. These are my own inventions.

Afterwards, Roo felt much better and said she was very keen to get up there.

That afternoon we went down to Walrus to stock up on provisions for our journey to find the polar bears. We spent a long time searching for the shops, as everything lay buried beneath the snow. Eventually we found the mailing station after Roo fell down the chimney.

I bought: a pair of wellies, some fish, cheese, candles and sausages.

Roo bought: a picture of a rabbit, an old bone and some jam labels.
I wish she wouldn't waste her money.

Afterwards, I played golf on the snow fields behind Walrus.
I found that golf kept my spirits up. I hit a good shot across
a glacier and the ball flew through the sky like a rocket.

When I got to where the ball lay I found a little penguin lying
in the snow. My ball had hit him on the head.

I put him in my golf bag and took him back to the cabin. Roo was very annoyed and said why didn't I invite the whole of the Arctic into our home and be done with it. We could fill the place with sea lions, Arctic foxes and sea birds and we could sleep outside!

HIP HIP HOORAY! And three cheers! The penguin woke up the next day and seemed much better.

He climbed all over my bed and wanted to get in with me. I liked the little fellow. Roo said he smelt of fish.

I planned our route on the map.
It would be a long walk to the
Great Bear Ridge.

Outside, the sky was changing
colours all the time. Something
very strange was happening.
I decided it was time for us
to set off.

We climbed high above the Gentle Slopes until we left Walrus far behind. Roo sped along and said she was in a hurry to reach the ice cream.

Halfway up the Great Bear
Ridge we pitched the tent and
crawled inside. We had a large
meal and went to sleep.

Disaster struck the next morning when a large gust of wind blew the tent away. We watched it float off over Blue Whale Bay. The wind started to blow harder. I tied us all to a rope so that none of us would blow away too.

We struggled on, but it was so windy. We eventually stopped and made an igloo. The wind grew more fierce and we had just finished the igloo when the storm hit.

It blew the trolley up into the air, taking Roo with it. I only just managed to pull her back down with my golf club.

But the trolley and everything else had gone.

We were so hungry and all our food had blown away. But then
Roo brought out the tin of macaroni that the captain had given
her. What a clever dog!

After eating it, we all huddled together in my sleeping bag to try
and keep warm. Meanwhile, the storm got more and more fierce.

Suddenly the
storm stopped. We
all crawled outside and
walked up the last bit to the
Great Bear Ridge. Roo ran ahead
like dogs do and when we got to the
top we saw the most beautiful sight …

The last polar bears were there, playing
with their cubs, rolling in the snow,
floating on icebergs.

And there too,
ice cream for Roo.